The Puppy Who Wanted a Boy

a Boy

by Jane Thayer

pictures by Seymour Fleishman

WILLIAM MORROW & COMPANY
NEW YORK 1958

WEEKLY READER

Children's Book Club

Edition, 1961

One day Petey, who was a puppy,
said to his mother, who was a dog,
"I'd like a boy for Christmas."

His mother, who was a dog, said she thought he could have a boy if he was a very good puppy.

So the day before Christmas Petey's mother asked, "Have you been a very good puppy?"

"Oh, yes!" said Petey. "I didn't frighten the cat."

"You didn't?" asked Petey's mother.

"Well-l, I just frightened her a *little*," said Petey. "And I didn't chew any shoes."

"Not *any*?" said his mother.

"Just a teeny-weeny chew," said
Petey. "And I remembered—well,
almost always remembered—to bark
when I wanted to go out."

"All right," said his mother. "I think you've been good for such a little dog. I will go out and get you a boy for Christmas."

But when Petey's mother came
back she looked very worried.
"How would you like a soft white
rabbit with pink ears for Christmas?" she said to Petey.

"No, thanks," said Petey.

"Don't you want a lovely ca-
nary?"

"I'd like a boy," said Petey.

"How about some guppy fish?
They're nice," said Petey's mother.

"I just want a boy," said Petey.

"Petey," said his mother at last, "there are no boys to be had."

"No boys?" cried Petey.

"Not one could I find. They're terribly short of boys this year."

Petey thought he couldn't stand it if he didn't have a boy.

Finally his mother said, "There now, there must be a boy some-where. Perhaps you could find some dog who would give his boy away."

No boys
ALL OUT OF BOYS
Sorry-no boys
NO MORE BOYS
NO BOYS TODAY

"Do you think I could?" asked
Petey.

"It wouldn't hurt to try," said
his mother.

So Petey hopefully started off.
It wasn't long before he saw a collie

racing with a boy on a bicycle.
Petey trembled with joy.

"If I had a boy on a bicycle,"
said Petey to himself, "I could run
like everything! I'll take a little run
right now, and I'll ask the collie

politely if he'll give his boy away."
So Petey leaped after the bicycle.
He called out to the collie, "Excuse
me. Do you want to give your boy
away?"

But the collie said *no*, he definitely *didn't*, in a dreadful tone of voice.

Petey sat down. He watched the collie, and his boy on a bicycle, until they were out of sight.

"I didn't really want a boy on a bicycle, anyway," said Petey.

After a while he saw a setter playing ball with a boy. Petey was

delighted. "If I had a boy to play ball with," said Petey, "I'd catch the ball smack in my mouth. I'd like to catch the ball now!"

But he remembered how cross the collie had been. So he sat down

on the sidewalk and called out politely, "Excuse me. Do you want to give your boy away?"

But the setter said *no*, he definitely *didn't*, in a terrifying tone of voice!

"Oh, well," said Petey, trotting off, "I don't think playing ball is so much fun."

Soon Petey came to a bulldog, sitting in a car with a boy.. Petey was pleased, for he was getting a little tired from so much walking.

"If I had a boy in a car," said
Petey, "I'd laugh at walking dogs.
I'd like a ride right now." So he
called out loudly, but very politely,
"Excuse me. Do you want to give
your boy away?"

But the bulldog said *no*, he definitely *didn't*, and he growled in Petey's face.

"Oh, dear!" said Petey. He hurried behind a house and stayed there until he saw the bulldog and his boy drive away.

"Well, who wants to go riding in a car? Pff! Not me!" said Petey, coming out from behind the house.

He thought he would just rest a

while, though. He had come a long way for such a little dog. He was limping a bit when he started off again. After a while he met a Scotty,

walking with his boy and carrying a package in his mouth.

"Now that is a good kind of boy!" said Petey. "If I had a boy to take walks with and carry packages for, there might be some dog biscuit or cookies in the package. I would like a cooky this minute!" He hadn't had a bite of lunch.

But he remembered how cross the collie and the setter and the bulldog had been. So he stayed across the street and shouted at the top of his lungs, but polite as could be, "Excuse me. Do you want to give your boy away?"

The Scotty had his mouth full
of package. But he managed to say
no, he definitely *didn't*, and he
showed his sharp teeth to Petey.

"I guess that wasn't the kind of boy I wanted either," said poor Petey. "But my goodness, where *can* I find a boy?"

Well, Petey trotted on and on.

But he couldn't find a single dog who would give his boy away. Petey's ears began to droop. His tail grew limp. His little legs were *very* tired. My mother was right, he

thought. There isn't a boy to be had.

Just as it was getting dark, he came to a large building on the very edge of town. Petey was going slowly by, when he saw a sign: *Orphans' Home.*

"I know what orphans are," said Petey to himself. "They are children who have no mother, and no dog to take care of them either. Maybe I could find a boy here!" He padded slowly up the walk of the Orphans' Home. He was so tired he could hardly lift his little paws.

Then Petey stopped. He listened. He could hear music. He looked through the window. He saw a lighted Christmas tree, and children singing carols.

Then Petey saw something else.
On the front steps of the Orphans'
Home, all by himself, sat a boy! He
was not a very big boy and he
looked lonely.

Petey gave a glad little cry. He forgot about being tired. He leaped up and landed in the boy's lap. Sniff, sniff went Petey's little nose. Wiggle, wag went Petey's tail. He kissed the little boy with his warm, wet tongue. How glad the boy was to see Petey! He put both his arms around the little dog and hugged him tight.

Then the front door opened and a lady looked out. "Why, here you

are, Dickie!" she said. "What is our
newest boy doing out here all alone?
Come on in to the Christmas tree."

Petey sat very still. The boy sat still. The boy looked up at the lady and down at Petey. Petey began to tremble. Would the boy go in and leave him?

"I'm not alone," said the boy. "I've got a puppy."

"A puppy!" The lady came and looked at Petey in surprise.

"Can he come too?" said the boy.

"Why," said the lady, "you're a nice little dog. Wherever did you come from? Yes, bring him in."

"Come on, puppy," cried the
boy. In they scampered!
A crowd of boys were playing

around the Christmas tree. They
rushed at Petey. They picked him
up and petted him.

Petey wagged his tail. He
wagged his fat little body. He
frisked about and kissed every one
of the boys.

"Can we keep him?" said one.

"Can we give him some supper?" said another.

"Can we fix him a nice warm
bed?" said a third.

"We will give him some supper
and a nice warm bed," said the lady.
"And tomorrow we will find his
mother and see if she'll let him
stay."

Petey knew his mother would let him stay. She knew how much he wanted a boy. "But won't she be surprised," said Petey to himself, with a happy little grin, "when I tell her I got *fifty* boys for Christmas!"